PETER PAN
the motion picture event

WELCOME TO NEVERLAND

By Kate Egan

Based on the Motion Picture Screenplay
by P. J. Hogan and Michael Goldenberg

Based upon the Original Stageplay and Books
Written by J. M. Barrie

HarperFestival®
A Division of HarperCollins*Publishers*

Taking a trip to Neverland?

I can tell you everything you

need to know.

My name is Peter Pan.

Let me be your guide.

These are my friends Wendy, John, and Michael Darling.

They had adventures in Neverland they will never forget!

You'll need to do a few things
before your journey begins.
Practice telling stories—
everyone in Neverland loves to hear them!
Wendy is especially good at telling stories.

Be sure to practice fighting.

Believe me, it will come in handy.

Pack light for your trip to Neverland.
What you wear while traveling
doesn't matter.
The Darling children wore
their pajamas!

But you must promise this:

You can't tell anyone where you're going.

Not even your parents.

To get to Neverland, you fly!

No, not on a plane.

Watch me!

Just close your eyes and think

happy thoughts.

One sprinkle of fairy dust,

and off we go!

Follow the stars—second to the

right and straight on till morning.

There are lots of places to stay
in Neverland.

They are probably different
from what you are used to.

Wendy has her own little house.

My friends the Lost Boys built it for her.

I live underground with the Lost Boys.

You must slide through a tree trunk
to get there.

Only a child can fit down the trunk.

We have lots of fun in Neverland.

My friends and I never worry

about grown-up things.

We like to prowl through the forest.

And we have lots of parties.

You're invited!

We will introduce you to everyone

and tell you everything you need to know.

For instance, the mermaids
can trick you and trap you
before you realize it.
You must be careful.

Fairies are not as cute as they seem.
They're so small they can have only
one feeling at a time.

This is Tinker Bell, my good friend.
When she gets mad, she forgets to
be friendly.

Lots of Indians live in Neverland.

This is Princess Tiger Lily.

She is a friend to the Lost Boys and me.

By accident, Tiger Lily led John and

Michael into some big trouble.

But everything worked out okay.

There are some terrible creatures here.
For instance, there is a crocodile with
sharp teeth and wicked claws.
But he doesn't want to eat *you*.

The crocodile is looking for a pirate.

But not just any pirate—this pirate:

Captain Hook.

Hook is the most feared villain in

Neverland.

He leads a crew of ruthless men.

He has a hook instead of a right hand!

That's because of me—

I cut off Hook's hand myself.

Now Hook wants revenge.

He's always looking for me.

That can make life a bit dangerous
for my friends and me.

John and Michael found this out
firsthand.

Hook captured them and took them
to his castle.

Wendy and I tracked them down.

I tricked the pirates into freeing

John and Michael.

But then I had to face Hook alone!

Our swords clashed and clanged.

Luckily, I escaped unharmed.

Hook then tried to get Wendy

to join the pirates.

He was very sneaky.

He pretended to be nice.

He even cooked dinner for her!

But Wendy is smart.

She wasn't fooled.

So Hook did what any pirate would do.

He made Wendy walk the plank.

Hook's crew thought that was
a good plan.

Tinker Bell and I flew to the
pirate ship in time.
Tink distracted the pirates while
I caught Wendy in midair!
Then all of our friends fought
all of the pirates.
It was a spectacular battle.

Michael even got his teddy bear

back!

(Smee, a pirate, had stolen it.)

Your trip to Neverland
might not always be easy.
Your trip to Neverland
might not always be safe.
But it will always be full of adventure.